The Amazing Minecraft Family

Book 2

By: Pixel Ate

Chapter 1

"I know what we're doing today." A huge grin spread across Dad's face. "We're going to go fishing!"

"Yes!" Kate said, fist bumping the air. "I was hoping you would say that!"

He looked at her, a tear welling up in his eye. "I have never been more excited to be your dad. I thought you hated fishing!"

Kate blushed. "Well, normally yeah, but I *need* to get a saddle!"

Dad's huge smile flattened, then quickly came back. "I'll take it!" He shrugged.

Jack laughed at the two of them. "I want to fish, too, but we'll have to take turns. I think we only have enough string to make a couple fishing rods."

"Wait," Kate said, eyes shining with excitement. "You already have string?"

Jack's mouth slowly turned up into a sly grin. "Oh yeah, we forgot to tell you! We had to fight through some spiders to get back here last night."

Kate threw her arms around her brother and squealed so loudly it hurt his ears. "Okay, okay, that's enough," he said, pushing her away. He wiped each shoulder off, as if he were making sure not too many sister germs remained.

Dad turned to the kids. "Okay, now that we have the whole day ahead of us, and a safe home…"

"Well not THAT safe," Jack interrupted. "A creeper could blow it up pretty easy still."

"Well it's safer than sleeping outside," Dad huffed. "Anyway, now that we have a home, why don't you tell your mother and me about crafting."

Mom clapped her hands. "Oh yes, please do! I desperately want to know. I love to craft!" She grinned at the kids like a dog waiting on a steak bone.

Jack thought about Mom's crafting room back home. A huge desk and drawers filled with all kinds of paper and fabric. Shelves lined the walls from the floor to the ceiling filled with colorful bits and bobs. She made it all, from scrapbooks to homemade chapstick and everything in between, even clothes. Jack chuckled at the memory of the hats Mom would make for Bruce.

Bruce chose that moment to rub up against Jack's leg. "Meow," he said. He figured Bruce did NOT miss the hats at all. He would always run and hide when Mom called for him with some new hat in her hand.

"Well, I'll help you two learn how to craft by showing you how to make a fishing rod," Kate suggested, and held her hand out to Jack. "Would you drop the string, please?" He did, and Kate grabbed two of them and dropped a few of her sticks.

Everything floated there in front of them and Dad bent over to pick up the supplies.

"Well, now what?" he asked. "I have them in my coldbar."

Kate and Jack exploded in laughter. "It's a HOTbar Dad!" Jack said, barely able to breathe.

Dad shrugged. "Hot bar, cold bar, taco bar, ice cream bar... I just want to know how to make a fishing rod!"

Kate moved to the small table in the corner of their one-room dirt home and waved her hand at it. "First, you open the crafting table," she said.

"That's not a crafting table!" Mom said, throwing her arms around and pointing at it as if Kate had personally offended her. "It's not nearly big enough. Are there even any drawers? Where will the scissors go? And the measuring tape? And *all* the craft supplies, for that matter?"

"Umm," Kate said, "it's not... you don't... you know what, just come over here and touch it."

Mom stood by Kate and touched the crafting table. "Oh my!" she said as she began looking at something only she could see. "There is so much here, how do I make it all?" She was excited, clapping her hands and bouncing on the balls of her feet.

"Don't get too excited just yet, those are only recipes. See the little slider there? Slide it over," Kate said.

"Oh no! Everything disappeared?"

"What's left is just the recipes for the things you have the ingredients for… mostly. You still see some other stuff, but if it's in red, you can't make it yet."

Mom made a quiet face as she looked at all the things the crafting table showed her. Then suddenly her face lit up with joy again. "There's a recipe for fabric!"

"Let me take a look at that," Dad said and activated the crafting table. "Huh, there sure is a lot of stuff in here. How do we even get all these ingredients? Where do we find them?"

"Yes, do tell!" Mom cheered.

Jack and Kate smiled at each other. They remembered their first time in Minecraft and how exciting it was to learn about all the things you could do. It had felt like they were in a whole other world, which, now they really were.

"Well," Jack said, "each ingredient is found pretty much right where you would think. The different kinds of stone are in caves, wood is in the forest, wool is on sheep…"

Mom frowned. "Oh dear, that's right. I really don't like the idea of killing anything." She looked down, sadness on her face.

Kate grabbed her hand. "I know you don't like that part, Mom, but this is for our survival. And remember, it's just a video game. And... it's not gruesome or anything."

"But sheep are so cute," Mom whined. "And this sure doesn't *feel* like a video game."

Jack smiled. "We can eventually make sheers to get wool from the sheep and that way you don't have to kill them."

Mom looked up at him. "That's great news! I know we'll have to kill animals at some point so we can eat, but I just can't bear the thought of it."

"If it helps," Jack said, "since we usually use a pickaxe, you can think of it as mining the animals instead." Mom gave Jack 'the look' and Jack knew it was time to go. "Well, gotta go! Lots and lots to explore!" He ran out the door before she could say anything else.

"Don't you mine any sheep young man!" she shouted after him.

"Meow," said Bruce as he darted out the open door.

Kate spent some more time showing Mom and Dad how to use the crafting table before finally making the thing she wanted most: a fishing rod. Well, it wasn't THE thing she wanted most. That would be a saddle, but since she couldn't just make one, fishing was the way to go.

The pole appeared in her hotbar and she immediately equipped it. A wooden stick appeared in her hand, with the hook swinging in front of the huge grin that had spread across her face.

"Now that I made my fishing rod, you can find me at the pond!" She left in such a hurry she almost snapped her brand new fishing rod on the door.

Dad looked at Mom and shrugged. "She must be excited."

"You know that one-track mind of hers! The only thing on that track is a horse."

Dad laughed and pulled her in for a hug. "What are you going to do today?"

"I'm going to gather ingredients to make some of this stuff." She waved toward the crafting table. "I think I'll start with wood since I already know how to get that, and it looks like you need it for a lot of recipes."

Dad nodded. "Well, I'm going to try my hand at fishing, too. A delicious fish dinner sounds good about now, doesn't it?" He rubbed his belly.

"Meow," Bruce said, peeking in from the hole in the ceiling, his ears fully perked up.

"How does he always know when we're talking about food?" Mom laughed. "Well you two have fun, Kate will love the company." She leaned in and gave Dad a kiss.

"Gross!" Jack said from his bed.

Mom and Dad both jumped higher than a cat scared of a cucumber. Jack laughed so hard he fell off the bed.

"Jack!" Mom shouted. "How did you get in here!?"

Jack's voice was muffled from under the bed where he had rolled while laughing. "You should have seen your faces!" He composed himself and sat back on the bed. "I respawned here after I died."

"What?!" Dad asked. "You died? Are there monsters around?" He ran to look out the door and quickly pulled it closed.

Jack stood up. "Oh, no, no monsters. It's daytime. Well, I mean some monsters are out in the day, like creepers and spiders and,"

"Jack, focus," Dad said. "What killed you?"

Jack held his hands up and shrugged. "I fell off a mountain."

His parent's mouths fell open in shock. "You... fell off... a mountain?" Mom asked, like she must have heard him wrong.

Jack shrugged. "Yeah, I was chasing a sheep to mine... er... pet, and it ran up a mountain. I guess I wasn't looking where I was going, and I fell right off the ledge. Anyway, gotta go!" He ran out the door, leaving it wide open again.

Mom and Dad just stared at the dust he left behind. "'I'm not sure how that boy will survive childhood," Mom said, shaking her head.

"So I guess it's a good thing he can respawn now?" Dad said. Mom eyed him then laughed. Dad chuckled back and kissed her cheek. "Well, I'm off to catch some fish!".

Chapter 2

Jack ran out of the house as fast as he could. He was excited to explore all around their new home. This time though, he would be a little more careful and NOT follow a sheep off a cliff. He was just so excited to be living in Minecraft!

No one had asked him, but Jack wasn't upset at all about being stuck in the game. He had told the truth when he said he didn't know how they got here. He really didn't, and it was definitely strange, but he was glad they were. Mom couldn't even tell them to log out!

Jack loved Minecraft. He loved building houses and fighting monsters and making weapons and exploring and... all of it! His favorite house was the one he had just built in the last world he and Kate played in.

They had finally figured out how to make glass and their house had a whole wall of windows. It was pretty cool looking. They had spent a decent amount of time playing the game, but there was still so much to learn and know. They had really only discovered the basics but had plenty of fun mining and making things.

He had heard about things like the Nether and the End from friends but hadn't ever gotten there yet. Or even close as far as he knew. He had too much fun mining and fighting. Now that he was IN Minecraft, he had all the time in the world! "This is SO COOL!" he shouted into the air. "I cannot wait to tell my friends!"

He ran across the plains looking for anything interesting, when he saw a few blocks of grass missing in the ground. He slowed and peeked over the edge into the hole. Jack smiled; it was just what he thought! Through the small, inconspicuous hole, he could see a massive cave system opening beneath the ground. Caves were a great place to find iron and coal!

He began digging stairs so he could enter the cave without splatting on the ground and having to face Mom again back at the house.

As soon as the stairs were done, he immediately began punching a rock. He was excited to have stone tools! He punched and punched and punched, but it seemed like it was taking longer than it did when he was playing from his couch with a controller.

Soon though, the block exploded into dust.

"Yes!" Jack shouted, then frowned. Where was his floating chunk of cobblestone? He wanted to make stone tools! He turned to look around then shrugged. He started punching another block of stone, and when it exploded, also leaving nothing behind, he stopped and smacked his forehead.

"Ugh, I need a tool to get cobblestone from this! Why didn't I make a wooden pickaxe before leaving the house?" He spun around to head back home, but the wide open mouth of the cave caught his eye.

"I'll just have a quick look," he said to no one, because no one else was there, before walking into the stone cavern.

The cave opened wide to a large room with surprisingly tall ceilings. The light poured in to the front of the room, but eventually filtered out, and towards the back of the area it looked pitch black.

Jack went in as far as he could see to look around. He found a few coal deposits which got him excited. With coal they could make a ton of different things!

He continued until it got so dark he couldn't see anymore. Which was precisely why he fell into a crack and plummeted so deep he lost track of where he was. He fell and fell until, with a loud CLUNK, he landed in a heap on the ground.

"Ow!" Jack moaned, and stood, brushing off his pants. He was down to a single heart and his whole health bar was shaking.

He sighed. He really didn't want to respawn again so soon after the last time. What would Mom say? He turned around hoping he wasn't going to be stuck in complete darkness.

Thankfully he wasn't. He seemed to have landed in another cave system. How deep in the ground was he? He had fallen a long way down.

Ahead of him was some faint light way off in the distance. With no other ideas, he shrugged and started walking towards the light.

The path there was a pain in the butt. Lots of climbing up and down, winding around and around, widening one-block holes so he could squeeze through. Finally, though, he made it to the source of the light.

In front of him was a stream of orange lava pouring out of the rock wall and flowing across the path of the cave towards another hole in the wall. "Oh man I love lava! I wish I had a bucket!"

He got close to the lava and put a hand near it. It was HOT. A lot hotter than it looked when he was just watching it on a screen. He was mesmerized by the gurgling red and orange liquid when something caught his attention. Something blue and shiny.

"Is that... diamond?" he said, his eyes widening in excitement. He couldn't quite be sure of it from where he stood, so he got dangerously close to the molten lava to get a better look.

Sure enough, directly above the stream of boiling hot lava, was a shiny light blue ore.

"It IS diamond! Oh man, Kate is gonna freak out!" Then *he* freaked out when he felt the sting of sharp fangs bite into his ankle.

"Ow!" He looked down to see a spider trying to eat him. He was down to half a heart.

Jack kicked at the thing, which in hindsight he realized it wasn't the best idea to take his only good leg off the ground, as he lost his balance and landed right in the lava. "Oh man!" was all he had time to say before the lava ate the last of his heart, sending him to respawn.

Chapter 3

Kate was wasting no time. She was going to fish up a saddle today no matter what! She couldn't wait to have her own horse.

As the pond came into view, she stopped to admire it. It was a pretty nice pond. Not too big, not too small. Along one edge was a sandy beach and the other sides were lined with grass and dotted with a few trees. It really was quite beautiful, with the clear blue water rippling in the sunlight, the fish swimming around, and the drowned wandering around on the ledge.

Her eyes widened. A drowned?! Oh man! Kate huffed and stomped her foot. She didn't want to deal with a drowned. They were zombies that had stayed in water too long and turned into something even stronger. She'd forgotten about them in her excitement to fish for a saddle.

She sighed and moved to a spot on the pond as far away from the gurgling monster as she could.

With an excited grin she rubbed her hands together then got her fishing rod ready and cast the bobber into the water. Not much later a trail of bubbles formed in the water and made its way closer to the bobber. This was it; she was one step closer to her dream.

She imagined herself, galloping on a horse, the wind in her face, her hair flowing behind her. She would train her horse to jump, and build an amazing horse arena like her friend Reagan and she had done in their very own 'Girls 10 and Older' world they played in. No boys were allowed, especially brothers.

With visions of an epic horse ranch dancing in her head, she completely forgot to reel the line in, and the bobber stopped moving. "What?" she asked as she realized what she had done. "Oh rats!" Now she would have to wait again.

"What's wrong?" a voice asked behind her and Kate jumped so high she almost fell in the water.

Dad chuckled; he had always liked to startle the kids. It was fun to watch them jump.

Kate windmilled her arms to keep from falling in the water and nearly lost her fishing pole in the process. "Don't DO that!" she yelled at him.

"Ahem," Dad said and raised an eyebrow at her. Kate blushed.

"Sorry, I didn't mean to yell at you. You startled me and almost fell in the water and lost my pole!"

"What made you upset? I mean, before I did."

"Oh it's nothing, I just missed my first catch."

He nodded. "Well let me tell you, I used to be quite the fisherman back in my day, maybe ole Dad can help you out." He elbowed his daughter. "What do you think? Want me to show you the ropes?"

It was Kate's turn to chuckle as she gestured towards the water. "Fishing here isn't like back home, Dad," she said. "It's way easier."

Dad made a face at her. "So easy you already messed up?"

She stuck her tongue out at him. "Watch this!" She cast her line out again, the bobber landing far out into the water. "Hey, nice cast!" Dad said. She couldn't help feeling proud, even though there was really no skill involved. But she wanted to impress her dad, so this time when the trail of bubbles came towards her bobber, she was going to pay better attention.

"What is that?" Dad asked, pointing to the trail of bubbles.

Kate smirked. "*That* is how fishing works here." She looked at her dad to find him studying the water intently.

"So bubbles just go over to your bobber and make it dance and then stop? Then what? How do you get the fish?" he asked.

Kate quickly turned to her bobber. She had missed it again! "Oh RATS!" she shouted even louder.

Dad laughed loudly this time, his whole body shaking. "Was it not supposed to do that?"

Kate growled but ignored him as she cast her bobber back out. The water bubbled again and she wasn't going to ake her eyes off it for anything! She focused in, blocking out everything that wasn't those bubbles.

The water trails got closer and closer, and finally her bobber dipped under the water!

She reeled her line in and Dad cheered. Kate was so happy, she glanced back at Dad who had a huge smile on his face. A smile that quickly changed to a look of shock at something behind her. She spun around just in time for the big, slimy fish she had caught to splat her right in the face! It caught her by such surprise that she fell over.

Dad laughed so hard he, too, fell onto his butt as Kate spluttered and wiped the fish smell off. She snatched up her catch, a raw cod, and put it in her inventory. Then she stood up, her hands on her hips, and glared at Dad. She was practicing 'the look' that Mom did.

It must have worked, at least a little, as Dad stopped laughing and stood up. "I'm sorry, Kate. It really wasn't very nice of me to laugh. That was just so funny!" He hugged her. "Thank you for showing me how to do it."

Kate blushed. "Anyway, it's really easy."

Dad laughed again and pulled out his own fishing rod he had made with the last two pieces of string. "Let's do it together and see what we can get, okay kiddo?"

Kate nodded, and with a smile, they both cast their lines into the pond.

Chapter 4

Mom sighed after Dad left. She was used to being alone at home every morning after Dad went to work and she shuttled the kids off to school. But this house was so dreary, and ugly and... dirty. It was made of dirt so that made sense, but she really wanted to fix it up.

"I need to get some wood so I can make plenty of sticks and... planks." She was proud of herself for remembering what they were called. Maybe if she made the house into a log cabin it would feel a little more homey and a whole lot less... dirt-y.

She left the house to go to the nearby trees and gather some wood. She passed the trees that Kate and she had punched down and shook her head. The trunks were gone, but the top of the trees stayed there, floating in the air. "This is such a strange place."

Mom got to work punching trees and gathering wood. Something in her just couldn't stand leaving the floating leaves so she punched them too. Deliciously sweet apples occasionally fell, and she munched on one as she worked, whistling a small tune.

The apple tasted *really* good. It was crisp and crunchy with a flavor that surpassed even the best apples she had ever tasted back home. The weird thing was *every* apple she got tasted this way. She knew because she couldn't stop eating them. They were just so good!

Mom kept working like this for a good long time, punching trees and collecting wood and apples. She noticed she never got tired as long as she kept munching an apple every now and then. She did get bored though and doubted there was any fruit for that.

She was on what felt like her hundredth tree, just punching away, and she had three full stacks of 64 oak logs and a full stack of apples, even though she kept eating them. She hoped that was going to be enough wood to do all the things they wanted to.

Finally, she was too bored to keep going so she stopped and looked around. She had cleared out a sizable chunk of the forest near their camp.

She was thinking about snacking on another apple when a noise behind her made her stop. She snapped around and saw a green and black armless creature coming straight towards her.

"Oh no you don't Mr. Creepy!" she shouted and started backing away.

Unfortunately, shouting was the wrong thing to do. The creeper homed in on her, opened its mouth wide and charged. Mom screamed and turned, running as fast as she could towards the camp.

"Help! Help!" she shouted as she got closer. She could just barely make out Dad and Kate, but they were on the other side of the pond — too far to help. She ran, and the creeper followed close on her heels. Mom tripped over a block of leaves that she had tossed out and the creeper got right up to her and started hissing and flashing.

"No!" Mom screamed and leapt to her feet to run. The creeper stopped flashing and started after her again. She was finally almost to the house and was screaming and waving her arms. Dad and Kate looked up with startled looks on their faces, and when they realized what was happening, they tossed their fishing poles and ran towards Mom.

Mom didn't know what to do so she simply ran in circles around the house. The creeper followed her relentlessly and she was getting annoyed. Didn't these things ever quit? Around and around she went, the creeper right after her.

On another pass around the house, Dad and Kate were close enough to shout at her, and Kate yelled something, but Mom could only make out one word.

"...house!" Kate yelled.

Mom thought she must have been telling her to go in the house, and she remembered from the night before how the monsters couldn't open the door. As the door came back into view, she threw herself toward it, opened it, and ran inside as quickly as she could, slamming the door behind her. She collapsed against it, breathing hard.

"Mom?" Jack said, freshly respawned from his accident in the cave. "What's going on?"

"Oh Jack!" she said, still catching her breath. "A creepy is after me!"

"A creeper?" Realization crossed over Jack's face. "Mom! Get away from the door!" he yelled and jumped towards er to help her up and away. Just as he grabbed her hand, he heard the telltale hiss from the other side of the door.

"Oh man, not again," Jack said just as the creeper exploded, blowing a massive hole in the house and the ground they stood on.

Chapter 5

Kate stood there, shaking her head. In front of her was the half-ruined house they'd been calling home. She and Dad had tried to tell Mom to stay away from the building so Kate could draw off the creeper and make it explode somewhere else, far away from anything important. "Stay away from the house!" she'd yelled, but Mom must have heard the wrong thing because she did exactly the opposite.

Dad had tried to get its attention by running up to the creeper, flailing his arms wildly and screaming like a fool, but instead he was blown up right along with it.

With three pops, Mom, Dad and Jack appeared inside what used to be the house. Only one of the beds remained, but they all respawned as if they were still there.

"Oh those darn creepies!" Mom said, stomping her foot. "I lost all my stuff again, and I spent so long punching trees!"

"It's okay," Kate said and gave her a hug to console her. "Your stuff should still be around here somewhere... what did you have?"

Mom looked all around at their poor broken house. It was a near total loss. Where minutes ago there had been a wall with a door that shut tight and kept them safe from monsters, was now nothing but a deep crater in the ground, the entire front half of the house just... missing. Only the back wall remained solid. The roof and two side walls were in various states of disarray, random holes dotting the stacked dirt blocks, like a second grader with many missing teeth. Cubes of debris floated all around.

"I had some wood, leaves, and apples," she said.

Kate began picking up the floating blocks. "How much wood?" she asked.

Mom also started cleaning up. "Three stacks of 64, I guess that's the most you can put in a slot. And I had almost a whole stack of apples."

Kate and Jack stopped cleaning and looked at each other. "Three stacks!?" Jack asked. "That's a ton! Good job, Mom!"

"Is it?" Mom asked. "I don't really know. I mean, I was out there for a while."

Jack laughed. "You must have been punching trees forever! Did you at least make an axe?"

"An axe?" Mom asked with her eyebrows pushed together.

For the second time Jack and Kate stopped and looked at each other.

"What is it?" Dad asked. "Did she do something wrong?"

Kate sighed. "I'm sorry, there are some things we really should have done first. Before I got all obsessed with getting a saddle."

Jack hung his head. "Yeah, I shouldn't have run off. I think we forgot how new you guys are to Minecraft."

"What do you mean?" Mom asked, a worried look on her face. "What did I do?"

Kate cleared her throat. "It's not what *you* did, it's what *we* didn't do. We should have told you about tools and made some with you. It would have saved you a ton of time in the forest."

Jack smirked. "And I probably wouldn't have respawned again if I had a pickaxe to use."

"Well, tell us now then," Dad said. "I love tools!"

While they continued cleaning the mess of their demolished home and collecting all the dropped loot, Kate and Jack told their parents about all the different tools they could make and what they were helpful for.

Working together they rebuilt the house in record time, this time using the wood Mom had collected. When it was finished, they stood back to admire their work. Mom had a huge smile spread across her face. This was so much better than a dirt home.

"Well, I certainly see what you mean about the first house being so weak," Dad said. "A creeper could never blow this up this beauty." He patted one of the walls.

"Well..." Jack said, his face scrunched up. "Creepers can pretty much blow up anything. But the stronger the material, the less it destroys."

"But I gathered all this wood!" Mom said, looking annoyed.

"Wood is usually the second step, Mom, you did good," Kate reassured her.

"But we should work on upgrading it even more," Jack added.

"Well how do we do that?" Dad asked.

"Oh, that's easy. Well, kind of easy," Jack said. "The best way would be to rebuild it out of stone." He pulled a wooden pickaxe from his inventory. "Take a pickaxe to some stone and start whacking away!"

"We should all work together," Kate said. "It will go a lot faster and we'll be safer too."

"Alright," Dad said. "How do we start?"

"We start with tools," Kate said, and made enough basic wooden tools out of Mom's leftover wood for the entire family.

"Then," Jack said, "we mine. We can start digging right outside."

"Right by the house?" Mom asked. "Is that dangerous?"

Kate shook her head. "No, it'll be fine. Jack and I always used to make a little mine right next to our houses so we would have some place to run if monsters appeared."

"Well what are we waiting for? Let's go!" Dad took out his new pick with a mighty swing, accidently knocking a block out of the wall. "Oops."

Immediately Bruce's face appeared through the new hole and jumped into the house. "Meow," he said before jumping onto a bed, circling a few times, laying down, and falling asleep.

"Well, I'm glad I could be of service to you, lazy cat," Dad said, and everyone laughed.

Chapter 6

In a short amount of time the family had a decent size mine going. They had dug into the ground, leaving a path of stones untouched as a stairway in and out. Occasionally Dad would dig straight up to pop a hole in the ceiling to let in some light.

It didn't take too long before they realized four people mining at the same time wasn't a great idea.

They realized this because they kept hitting each other with the pickaxes. Jack's pickaxe in Kate's arm, Mom's pickaxe in Dad's back. Mostly it was Jack, though. He got a little crazy with his pickaxe and ended up hitting everyone else at *least* twice. Before anyone could be sent to respawn, Dad and Kate kicked him out of the mine, and put him in charge of using the cobblestone they gathered to remake the house. Mom followed him to supervise.

Dad and Kate mined, popping rocks to get cobblestone, and Dad was having a great time. "This is a lot of fun," he told Kate. "Your old dad isn't too bad at survival, eh?"

Kate forced a laugh. "Yep, mining is alright," she said, "though I prefer making animal pens and designing a farm."

Dad nodded. "That sounds like you, you always have loved animals." He popped another brick, then stopped, looking into the hole he had made. "Uhhh... Kate... what's this?" he asked, pointing into the hole.

Kate stopped hitting rocks and looked in. A few blocks were dotted with dark spots. "Oh, that's coal, when you mine you can find all kinds of different blocks. Coal, Iron, Gold..."

"GOLD!?" Dad shouted and Kate had to cover her ears. Dad cleared his throat. "Oh, ahem, sorry about that. You can find gold?"

Kate smiled. "Yeah you can find gold and diamonds even."

Dad's face lit up like he had just swallowed a glowstone block. "Oh, I am for *sure* going to find some diamonds," he whispered.

Kate just shook her head. "They are really, really deep, you'll have to dig for a long time."

Without another word Dad started mining faster than Kate thought possible. Rocks were flying every which way. "Hey!" Dad said suddenly as he stopped.

"What is it?" Kate asked.

He held up a broken stick. "My pick broke!"

"Yeah, they do that. You should probably make one out of all that stone you've been collecting."

Dad scrunched up his face and looked at her. "Make a pick out of *stone*?"

Kate nodded. "Stone picks work faster than wood ones, too."

Dad looked at his broken stick. "A stone pick, and it's even faster..." he looked at Kate. "That ROCKS!"

Kate just stared at him.

"Get it?" he said with a huge cheesy grin. "Use a stone pick to mine rock…" He started laughing at his own joke, slapping his knee.

Kate sighed. "Ooookay Dad." She rolled her eyes and began picking up all the cobblestone and coal that had fallen to the ground.

"Your old man is pretty funny!" Dad said after he finally took a breath. "We should probably go check on Mom and Jack and make some stone picks while we're up there."

Jack and Mom had been hard at work. He would cover one of the walls with cobblestone, and Mom would be inside the house, taking down the wood blocks. This had the benefit of making the house more secure, but also a little bigger.

Mom hummed a little song as she went, very happy to have a proper looking home, and even happier to have the dirt gone. "Looking good, Mom!" Kate said when she came in.

"Great job, Mom!" Dad said as he looked around.

"What are you all doing in here? Wipe your feet!" Mom demanded.

Jack shut the door as he came in behind them. "But... the floor... is dirt?" He pointed at the floor, but realized it was probably best to not argue. "It's nearly nighttime Mom didn't you notice?"

Mom's jaw dropped and she looked out the window, the sun was setting and it was getting darker. "Oh my! I was having so much fun I didn't realize how fast time went!" Jack and Kate shared a look; they knew very well how fast time could go in Minecraft. "We should settle in for the night," Mom said.

The sun set and with it the house turned dark. "Well, I guess since we can hardly even see in here, there is nothing left to do but go to bed," Mom said.

Jack smacked his forehead. "Oh, I can help with that." He went to the crafting station and a few seconds later came back with a block that was grey like cobblestone but had two holes in the front. He placed it in a corner of the room and activated it.

Suddenly the room lit up with light as fires came out of the bottom hole. The light died away, and Jack pulled out omething lumpy and black. A few seconds later, four torches appeared in his hand and he placed one on the wall. The area around the torch lit up brightly, fading the further it got from the source.

Mom and Dad gasped.

"What is THAT?!" Dad asked, pointing towards the furnace.

"It's a furnace," Kate said. "You can use it to smelt things or cook food."

Dad's face lit up brighter than the torch. "Wait a minute... You mean this is the thing-a-majiggy I can Barbecue with?!"

Dad rushed everyone to bed so he could have enough daylight the next day to get his barbecue on. "No more talking! No more moving! How do you turn this torch off?" He batted at it with his hand, blew on it, and when the fire wouldn't go out, he eventually just ripped it off the wall. Blackness fell over their small stone house.

"Goodnight," he said as he kissed their foreheads and tucked them all into their beds. Even Mom.

Chapter 7

Just as the sun rose the next day, Dad leapt out of his bed and ran to the furnace. He messed with it a bit before rushing over and dumping Jack out of his bed. "HEY!" Jack yelled as he hit the floor, still half asleep.

"Oh good, you're awake," Dad said.

Jack rubbed his butt that he had landed on. "You woke me up!"

"ANNNNYYYway, how do I work this barbecue?" Dad pointed at the furnace.

Jack rolled his eyes. "It's a furnace Dad, not a barbecue."

"Whatever, how do I work it?"

Jack sighed and stood up. "First you need some fuel, coal or-"

"Got it!" Dad held up a stack of coal.

Jack chuckled. "Okay, so you put the coal in, just like with the crafting table, then add the meat and presto, it starts cooking."

Mom and Kate were sitting up in bed now, yawning. Jack and Dad were so loud!

"Well darn it! I don't have any meat."

"Oh no," Mom said, "don't even think about it."

Dad looked at her. "What?"

Mom pointed her finger right at his nose. "I know what you're thinking! Don't you dare go mining any animals!"

"Delicious animals," Dad corrected her with a tilt of his head.

She put her hands on her hips. "Now you listen, we have plenty of apples to eat, and they work just fine for our food bars. We don't need to mine helpless animals."

Dad crossed his arms. "Now honey, I know how you feel about violence, but I really need you to hear me out on this. It's very important."

Mom raised her nose in the air. "What is so important?"

Dad smiled. "Barbecue."

Mom looked at him and raised an eyebrow.

"Barbecue?" Dad whined.

Mom rolled her eyes and shrugged. "Ugh, fine. Just don't tell me anything about it."

Dad ran over and swooped Mom up in a huge hug, swirling her around the room. "Barbecue!" He squealed and kissed her. "Now get out of here." Mom shoved him toward the door. "Jack, you go with him."

Jack, who was busy making gagging noises because his parents had just kissed, jumped up. "You got it, Mom! C'mon Dad, let's go!"

Dad headed towards the door but stopped just short of opening it. "Do we need anything, Jack?" he asked. "We want to be prepared."

Jack shook his head. "Nope, we can get whatever we need out there."

"Perfect!" Dad said and he opened the door for Jack, who led the way out.

Mom looked at Kate who was smiling at everything that had just happened. She shook her head and opened her mouth to say something, when the door opened just a bit and Dad's head popped in. "Barbecue!" he said and disappeared again.

Kate laughed and fell backwards onto the bed. "Boys are so weird!"

Mom laughed as well. "They sure are."

Chapter 8

"Well, Jack my man, which way to the meat?" Dad asked as they walked away from their house.

It was first thing in the morning, and the bright square sun was still rising into the sky. In front of them was the sparkling pond and beyond that, open plains, grass blocks as far as the eye could see.

Jack looked around, trying to decide which way to go. There were still quite a few trees to one side, their tall, block leaves blowing gently in the wind. The brown craggy mountains stood to their right.

Jack pointed and off in the distance to some sheep near the mountains. "We could get those."

Dad looked at him and frowned. "I was kind of hoping for a steak first."

Jack and Dad looked all around but didn't see any cows. "We could probably find a cow in the plains up ahead, if you wanted to do some exploring," Jack said, "but if we go for the sheep, it'd be much faster. Plus, you can get mutton and wool, which Mom might like."

"I don't think Mom would like mutton, she thinks sheep are too cute."

Jack laughed. "No, I mean she might like the wool! You can use it to make all kinds of things for decorations."

"Now Jack, that's my smart boy." Dad ruffled his hair. "If we bring her back some wool, maybe she won't be mad about the meat."

"We should probably make some swords then," Jack said. "If we just try to punch the sheep, it'll take forever."

Dad frowned. "Why didn't you say anything in the house then? We had our crafting table there and could have made tools. Now we have to go all the way back."

Jack just smirked at him. "Dad, one of the things you need to learn about Minecraft, is a good player is never without resources." He dug around in his inventory and pulled out one of the stacks of wood he had collected as they replaced the wood of the house with cobblestone.

In a mess of movement, he had turned some of the logs into planks, and a few moments after that, created a crafting table and set it down. Jack quickly made a wooden shovel, dug a little bit until he hit stone, and using a pickaxe he pulled out of his inventory, mined a bunch of rock.

Dad watched the whole time, his smile getting bigger and bigger. Eventually, Jack was done and had made four stone swords. He gave two of them to Dad with a flourish.

"Wow son, you're right, I do have a lot to learn about Minecraft. That was very resourceful how you could simply make us what we needed." He fist bumped Jack.

Jack grinned hugely, happy to make his Dad proud. "I just wanted to show you how easy it is to do stuff here," he said. "And with just a little knowhow, you can pretty much make whatever you need, wherever you are. Now what do you say we go get those sheep?"

Dad nodded towards the fluffy block animals. "Lead on!"

Jack took off like a rocket and Dad had to run to catch up with him. Soon they made it to the closest sheep and Jack immediately hit it with his sword. The sheep flashed red and ran off. "After it!" Jack yelled and began chasing the sheep.

Dad was caught off guard and followed Jack a little behind him. The sheep ran into some trees and Jack smacked face first into the trunk of one. Dad ran after the sheep and swung his sword, the sheep flashed red again and dodged around another tree. Jack met the sheep there, though, and in a final blow the sheep was down.

In a puff of dust the sheep fell to its side and disappeared, leaving behind a floating white cube and red hunk of meat. "We did it!" Jack yelled and stopped to dance.

"Put your sword away," Dad said. "You'll poke your eye out dancing with it like that." He bent over to scoop up the cube of wool and the meat. When he stood back up he had a crazy look on his face as he held out the piece of mutton. "Baaaaarrrbeeecuuuuueee," he said slowly.

"Let's get some more!" Jack said and ran off to the other sheep they had seen.

Dad put the meat in his inventory and chased after him. "Jack, wait up!"

Jack was just about to hit the other sheep with his sword when Dad stopped him. "Wait!" he shouted. "Let me get to the other side of it, then when you hit it and it turns to run, I can be there, sword at the ready. We should work smarter, not harder."

Jack paused a moment then shrugged. "Go for it." Dad moved into place, and like clockwork the two of them took out another sheep, gaining mutton and wool. "Great idea Dad," Jack said. "That was way better than chasing it all over."

"And running into a tree?" Dad asked.

"Yeah." Jack Jack rubbed his aching nose. "Way *way* better than running into a tree."

The two of them walked back towards the house, keeping their eyes peeled for any other tasty animals. All they found, though, were a few chickens which did not make Dad upset at all. "I love barbecued chicken!" he said as he happily collected the floating raw chicken. They also found a few eggs strewn about where the chickens had been walking.

Jack collected the eggs and grabbed the feathers, too. "I think I can make arrows with these," he said. "I want a cool bow and arrow set!"

"Just don't let your Mom see," Dad said with a smirk.

Jack agreed that was probably a good idea. "Hey Dad, want to see something cool?" he asked.

"Sure son, what's up?"

Jack hacked away at some grass that was close by and collected the floating seeds. He continued slashing at the grass, wanting to quickly gather as many as he could.

"Um, cutting grass doesn't seem that cool. In fact, I did it all the time back at home and I never once thought to myself, 'this is cool!'"

Jack rolled his eyes. "Patience is a virtue, Dad."

"Ah, so you do listen."

Jack rolled his eyes again. When he was satisfied with his seed collection, he waved Dad to follow him and they wandered around briefly until they came across another chicken. Jack put his sword away and held the seeds in his hand.

The chicken clucked and saw them, then the seeds, and instantly locked onto Jack like he was the chicken's best friend. Wherever Jack went the chicken followed him. If Jack ran, the chicken ran. If Jack zigged and zagged, the chicken zigged and zagged. Jack did a few silly little maneuvers going up and over blocks, and round and round in circles, and the chicken followed, always right at his heels.

Dad was off a way, bent over in laughter. "That's too funny!" he managed to say between heaving breaths. He started hacking some grass to gather seeds of his own. With handfuls of seeds, and a chicken each, they walked the rest of the way home, chickens in toe.

When they got home Dad slammed the door open and shouted in a sing-song voice, "Honey! I'm home!" and strolled in.

Mom looked up at him with a sweet smile on her face, which instantly morphed into shock and then anger as Jack and the two chickens followed in behind.

"WHY ARE THERE CHICKENS IN THE HOUSE!?"

Chapter 9

Dad put his seeds away and his chicken shadow immediately started flapping and jumping all over the place. "No chickens in the house!" Mom shouted and chased after the bird, shooing it away. The chicken darted o the bed, and Mom jumped after, but she had leapt so fast und the bed was so bouncy that when she landed, she pounced right off, flailing and landing hard on the floor.

All the sudden out of nowhere, like a bolt of black and white lightning, Bruce zipped in and charged at the chicken, smacking it with his claw. The chicken flashed red and went crazy flapping and clucking and leaping trying desperately to get away from Bruce Lee the Scar-Faced Ninja Attack Kitty From Japan (Who Smells Like Poop.)

The chicken landed on Kate's head but leapt off when Bruce jumped at it, sending several feathers flying. Bruce landed right on Kate's and she screamed as Bruce used her face to spring off after the chicken. Kate fell on her butt, a feather stuck in her hair and a dirty paw print on her forehead.

"Bruce! Knock it off!" Jack shouted.

"MEOW!" Bruce said and it looked very much like he was not planning on knocking it off, as he licked his lips while he continued to chase after the chicken. The chicken ran between Dad's legs and he bent over to grab it, but Bruce darted in after, and collided with his head, knocking him to the ground. "Ack, ya darn cat!" Dad yelled from the floor.

Bruce leapt in the air and it looked like he was finally going to catch the chicken as it fled out the door. Jack moved just a little quicker, though, and slammed the door shut after the bird, Bruce landing face first into it and sliding to the ground. The cat spun around and eyeballed the other chicken who was oblivious to everything that had just happened, happily pecking at the seeds Jack had dropped on the ground.

"Meow," Bruce said and got into pouncing position, his tummy low to the ground with his butt in the air wiggling and the tip of his tail flicking back and forth. Just as he jumped, Mom, who had finally gotten herself back up, snatched him in midair. "Meow?" Bruce whined.

Mom poked her finger in his nose. "Be nice to chickens!"

"Meow," Bruce said.

She put Bruce under her arm and pointed at Dad, her eyes squinty and serious. "You two, get those chickens out of here, and I had better never see them inside again!"

"Okay, okay," Jack said with his hands held out. "Why don't you like chickens, Mom? They're so funny!"

Mom held Bruce out like a loaded weapon at Jack, who opened the door to help Dad get the other chicken out of the house. "Because," Mom said, "they poop all over the place, and I don't want chicken poop on my bed!"

Kate followed Dad and Jack out the door but stopped to look at Mom. "Uh, haven't you noticed yet? There's no pooping in Minecraft."

Mom opened her mouth to say something then closed it as she realized Kate was right.

Kate shut the door with a giggle and followed Dad. "Hey, wait up!" she called to him and Jack.

Jack, who had pulled out more seeds and had both of the chickens following him around was laughing as he went in circles. "It's a chicken parade!"

Kate rolled her eyes. "Let me make a pen and we can raise them, Jack."

Dad looked at her. "Kate, sweetie, I don't think Mom wants us to have chicken pets."

Kate, who had already started making a wall of dirt two blocks high, kept working. "Not as pets Dad. Well, only kind of. Chickens are good food, and we can breed them to make as many as we want."

"Oh, your mom DEFINITELY doesn't want that," Dad argued.

Kate laughed. "I know, but we have to eat, and I'm already tired of apples. She keeps force-feeding me them, even though I'm not hungry!"

Jack walked over to Kate and into the makeshift pen she had made. "We should really make this out of fencing," he said, eying the dirt wall.

Kate nodded. "Yeah, but for now let's just get these chickens locked up."

"Okay," Jack said, "get ready to put some blocks up!" Just as he was about to leave, he gave one of the chickens some seeds and a heart puffed up and appeared above the chicken's head. He repeated this with the other chicken until it, too, had hearts above it.

The two chickens stood next to each other and in a moment, a little baby chicken poofed into existence. "It's so cute!" Kate squealed.

Jack ran out the pen and Kate quickly placed two dirt blocks, completing the pen, and locking the chickens inside. "Perfect!" she said. "Now we can have chicken whenever we want, plus we'll get eggs."

"And feathers!" Jack said. "Pew pew pew! I'm going to make a bow!" He pulled his arm back as if he were pulling a bow string.

Kate dusted off her hands and looked at Dad. "Can we *please* finally get some fishing in now?

Chapter 10

"Oh! I want to go fishing too!" Jack said.

"Alright, we only have two fishing rods, so we'll have to take turns," Dad said.

"You guys can take turns; I'm getting that saddle!" Kate said with her hands on her hips.

"That's not fair!" Jack stuck his tongue out at her.

Dad held his hand up. "That's enough of that you two. Jack, you can share with me, Kate really wants to try for a saddle. She has a big goal, and we will support her in that."

"Ugh, fine, but I go first."

"Nope," Dad said. "Dad's first." He turned to go towards the pond.

"Okay," Jack said, with a twinkle in his eye. "But didn't you want to try barbecuing?"

Dad stopped mid step, his foot still in the air. Barbecue... I forgot!" He threw the fishing rod at Jack. HereyougohavefunIloveyou!" He shoved passed the kids, running back to the house so quickly that Jack was knocked over and fell to the ground.

He stood up and collected the fishing rod. "Ready Kate?" he asked, but Kate wasn't there. He quickly looked around and saw she was almost to the pond. "Hey! Wait!" Jack ran up to her. "Why did you ditch me?"

Kate blew out a breath, "I didn't ditch you. I'm literally just going right over here."

"Hmph," Jack said as they got to the edge of the water. "I bet I catch more fish than you!"

"I don't even care," Kate said as she prepared her fishing rod. "I'm not here for the fish."

"Right, a saddle," Jack said and they both cast their lines into the water. They waited and soon bubbles formed and flowed towards Jack's bobber. It went under the water, but Jack wasn't fast enough and caught nothing.

Kate chuckled. "You won't catch more than me if you keep doing it like that."

Jack made an angry face at her. "I thought you weren't in it for the fish?"

Bubbles formed and made a path towards Kate's bobber this time. She eyed them intensely, determined not to miss. "I'm not, but I still want to win." Her bobber sank under and she pulled back on the fishing rod. She pulled and pulled, her rod bending tremendously.

"Jack! I think I got a huge one!" she said and pulled on it again. Jack watched as her rod bent further and further, looking as if it might snap in half, as she tried to pull out whatever it was she had caught.

"Wow, it must be a huge one!" Jack moved over to help her. With both of their hands on the fishing rod, they pulled and pulled and pulled until they finally saw something bubbling at the surface.

"Pull harder! It's almost up!" Kate said, excited and hopeful that maybe she had caught her saddle. With a huge final heave, the water broke, revealing a drowned with a trident!

"AHHHH!!!" Kate screamed, shocked at the creature at the end of her pole.

The drowned clambered onto some rocks in the water and threw its trident at Kate, but Jack dove and tackled her to the ground just as it was about to hit. "Kate! Pull it out of the water!"

Her fishing line had gotten tangled on the creature's arm, and that had been what she was pulling up. Too bad it wasn't the drowned's throwing arm as it threw another trident, this time hitting Jack. "OOOOOF!" he said as a huge chunk of his hearts vanished in an instant.

The drowned was reaching back to throw again, but Kate yanked on her fishing rod hard enough that it disrupted its aim. The trident flew way off course, and straight through the window of the house. "Ouch! My butt!" they heard Dad yell from inside.

"What in the world!?" Mom shouted and must have dropped Bruce who darted out the open window.

"Meow," Bruce said.

Jack and Kate continued yanking on the fishing line, trying to get the drowned out of the water. It was strong, though, and threw another trident, hitting Kate in the shoulder. "Ouch!" she yelled, accidently dropping the fishing rod. "Nooo! My rod!" she yelled as the drowned moved further into the water. It stopped and threw a trident again, hitting Jack as he tried to push Kate towards the house.

"Come on Kate, we gotta get out of here, it's too strong in the water!"

"But my rod fell in the water!" she shouted.

"Just leave it!" he yelled back and gave Kate a shove away from the pond. She stumbled but caught herself and with a growl ran back to the house. Jack started after her, but another trident caught him and he poofed back to the respawn point.

Chapter 11

"What on earth is going on out there?" Mom asked Jack after he respawned in the house. Jack opened his mouth to answer when the door slammed open and Kate, angry enough to cook an egg on her head, stormed in.

"RUTTON SUTTON DROWNEDS!" she screamed.

"Kate!" Mom said. "Don't use that kind of language!"

"But Mom!" Kate argued. "A drowned stole my fishing rod!" Her anger melted into sadness and she rushed to Mom, who hugged her tight. "I just wanted to fish for a saddle so I could finally have my own horse." A tear came out of her eye.

"Shh, it's okay, dear," Mom said as she patted Kate's back. "Dad will help you get another one, won't you honey?" She said this last part to Dad who was squatting down, intensely watching the furnace. "WON'T YOU DEAR!?" Mom said a little louder.

Dad jumped and looked around the room. "Huh? What? Sorry, I was watching the meat cook. What's going on?"

"Kate had her fishing rod stolen by a drowned. You need to help her get it back, and maybe teach it a lesson about taking things that don't belong to you," Mom said.

"Hey! What about me!?" Jack said. "It respawned me!"

"Did you lose a fishing rod too?" Mom asked.

"Well yeah, when you get sent to respawn you lose all your stuff."

"Wait a minute!" Dad stood up with his arms crossed. "You mean to tell me you lost the fishing rod I let you borrow? *My* fishing rod?"

Jack's mouth fell open and he looked from his Dad to his Mom, who was still consoling Kate. "Wha...bu..."

"That's no way to treat something I let you use Jack," Dad said.

Jack threw his hands in the air. "It's probably still out there! Floating right next to the pond. You'll just have to ght a drowned for it." He, too, crossed his arms over his chest.

"So is that where this thing came from?" Dad grabbed a trident from the floor. "I thought you were just playing a joke on me."

"There was no joke, there's an underwater trident-throwing zombie out there who hit you with that right before he took all my hearts with another one," Jack said.

Dad got a serious look on his face. "Well, I am just going to have to go down to that pond and deal with it, then aren't I? Water zombie or not, no one messes with my kids."

Mom smiled. She loved when Dad was a fierce protector. "Thank you dear," she said and kissed him on the cheek.

Dad nodded at her. "Right after my meat is done cooking."

"What!?" Mom and Kate said together, both standing in front of him with hands on their hips.

Dad looked back. "It's barbecue! I can't overcook it!"

Jack fell to the floor he was laughing so hard.

Mom pointed her finger at Dad. "You better go help your children with their bully right *now*." She didn't yell it, which was even more scary than if she would have. Instead she used her 'Don't mess with Mom' voice and that was enough to make anyone obey.

Dad gestured at the furnace. "But, but... barbecue..." He stopped, the look on Mom's face sharper than the trident that hit him in the butt. "Okay dear," he said and stood up.

"Oh, thank you honey," Mom said to him, her voice sweet like honey now.

Kate ran up and gave Dad a hug. "Thank you, Daddy!"

Dad sighed, took another look at the furnace, and started towards the door. "Come on Jack, you're going to give me a hand."

Jack jumped up, looked at Mom, and didn't even think twice. "Okay Dad!" he said as he ran out the door.

When they were outside Dad closed the door behind them. "So Jack, how do we handle these drowned things?"

They started walking towards the pond. "Well, it will try really hard to stay in the water, because on land they light on fire," Jack said. "But we could go underwater and fight it."

"That doesn't sound easy," Dad said.

"It probably won't be. They are really tough, and they hit hard when they throw their tridents."

"Well, how can we get it out of the water?"

"I don't know if we can," Jack said, "they really don't like being on fire."

Dad gave Jack a look.

Jack smirked. "Okay, well, Kate's fishing line got wrapped around this one, so if we can get the rod, we might be able to pull it out of the water."

Dad snapped his fingers. "Great idea! We'll lure it up to the edge, then grab the fishing rod and pull it out. Then we can whack it with swords too!" Dad put his hand on Jack's shoulder. "Jack, you get to be bait."

"Wait, what? Why me?" Jack asked.

As they got close to the edge of the pond Dad stopped to look in. "Because," he said, "I'm stronger than you and can pull it out easier." Then he pushed Jack into the water. "Now hurry and lure it over, I want to be back before my barbecue is overcooked!"

Chapter 12

Jack spluttered in the water and shot Dad a dirty look. He hoped the barbecue DID burn. Well not really, Dad actually made really good barbecue and Jack thought it sounded delicious right about now.

With a sigh that sent bubbles to the surface, he started swimming. The pond was not huge, but it did have one really deep point. He figured if the drowned was going to be anywhere, that's where it would be. He swam slowly and saw it, standing at the deepest part of the pond. He swam up to refill his air then with a shake of his head, dove down.

The drowned saw him as he got close and turned to attack. Jack had been expecting it and moved just enough to dodge the thrown trident. He moved in as fast as he could through the water and punched the drowned one time, right in the nose. It flashed red and attacked back, this time hitting Jack as he swam away.

Jack took evasive maneuvers, swimming in all kinds of wild directions, up, then down, then zig, then zag, but all towards Dad at the side. The drowned was fast though and caught up to him, poking him with the trident. Jack's health was getting low, but he was really close to Dad. Thankfully, the drowned did significantly less damage poking him with the trident than it did throwing it.

Finally, Jack got to the edge and Dad reached in and grabbed him by the hand, yanking him out of the water in one fell swoop. The drowned followed, getting as close as it could while keeping its legs in the water and chucked another trident at them. Dad threw Jack out of the way and dove in to snag the fishing rod that was dangling from the drowned's arm.

"Ouch!" Dad yelped as he was poked by the trident. Then he smiled as his fingers clasped the rod and he jumped out of the water, pulling as hard as he could once his feet were on shore. The drowned took a step, then another as Dad pulled. "Jack! Come help!"

Jack darted over and pulled on Dad, who pulled on the pole, which pulled on the drowned. They yanked hard one last time and the drowned popped out of the water. The creature stopped attacking and scrambled to get back in he pond, but Dad and Jack held fast and soon it burst into lames.

They shielded their eyes as the fire burned bright in ront of them. "Jack!" Dad shouted, "use your sword!"

"On it!" Jack equipped his stone sword and whacked the lrowned until it poofed away. With the tension gone on the ine, Dad slammed backwards to the ground, flipping completely over.

"Whoa!" he yelped.

Jack did a little dance. "We did it! We did it! We beat the lrowned!"

Dad jumped up and began cheering also. "Oh yeah! We lid it!" Then he suddenly stopped and sniffed. "My barbecue!" He ran towards the house as fast as he could.

Jack rolled his eyes and collected all the items that were floating. When he was done, he looked out over the pond. He was happy about the place he had found for the family to use as a base, but he didn't want to have to deal with drowneds all the time.

He thought hard about it, trying to remember everything he could about drowneds. They didn't like being out of the water in daylight but would attack on land at night. They dropped tridents, a really cool weapon, and sometimes you could even get rare things from them. They HATED baby turtles and turtle eggs, and... "That's it!" Jack lit up with excitement. He remembered that they needed deep water to spawn!

He looked in his inventory and saw that he still had a ton of leftover cobblestone, so he knew what he had to do. He waded out into the water and went back over to the deepest part of the pond, swimming down. He grabbed a stack of cobblestone and started placing.

He had to swim back up and catch his breath but dove right back down again. He repeated this a few times before he finished and swam out of the pond. He looked down, pleased that he'd filled in the deepest part and had made the rest of the pond all level. It almost looked like a swimming pool now!

Jack was worried that they might not be able to fish in it anymore, so he brought out his fishing rod and cast it into the water. He didn't have long to wait before bubbles came to the surface and made their way to his bobber. With a quick jerk on the line, a fish came sailing out of the water straight towards him.

Jack smiled hugely. He had caught a tropical fish- the rarest fish in the game! Jack held out his hand to grab it, but a furry black shape came sailing through the air, claws out, to skewer the fish. "Meow!" Bruce said as he landed on top of his prize.

"Hey cat!" Jack yelled. "That's MY fish!"

Bruce looked at Jack, then the fish, then Jack again. "Meow," he said and started eating it.

"Darn cat."

Chapter 13

Jack walked back to the house, happy with what he had accomplished. Minecraft was great because you could just DO so much stuff. Want to build a house in a day? Done. Want to dig out a huge mine all the way down to bedrock? No problem. Want to fill in a pond so your family can have a safe place to swim and fish? Easy peasy.

When he got to the door a smell greeted him that made his mouth water. He went inside and the smell was so strong it filled entire house. Mom and Kate were sitting on the beds waiting with an eager look on their faces. Dad was looking out the window.

"JACK!" he shouted, "Jack come-"

"I'm right here Dad," Jack said.

Dad jumped into the air, startled, and bonked his head on the top of the window frame. "Ow!"

Kate giggled and Dad rubbed the top of his head. "Jack! Guess what's ready?"

Jack came in and sat on his bed. "Barbecue?"

"BARBECUE!" Dad shouted and pulled the piping hot food from the furnace. He handed each of them a cooked mutton. "I've never made this before, and it was weird cooking it in this thing," he waved at the furnace, "and I don't have any sauce... but I sure hope it's good!"

They all held the cooked mutton and Dad looked at them expectantly. His eyes were wide as he gestured for them to eat. One by one they took a bite. "Oh, it's tasty!" Mom said.

Jack took a bite, a smile on his face. "It's real good, Dad!"

Kate ate the whole thing in one go. "Yummy!"

Dad grinned hugely and ate his. "It IS good! I'm so glad I can barbecue here." A single tear formed in his eye.

"We are too," Kate said, licking her fingers.

Mom nodded her head and stood up to give him a hug. "It was delicious honey. The only problem..." Dad lifted his head to look at her with a worried look on his face. "Is that we are not supposed to be eating here. We'll get crumbs in the bed!"

Jack and Kate looked at each other and rolled their eyes then laughed. "What?" Mom asked. "We need to get some furniture and eat at a table like civilized people, not savages." She crossed her arms and nodded her head like she knew she was right and nobody could convince her otherwise.

Kate stood up. "Well it's getting dark, should we get ready for bed? We've got a big day tomorrow."

Dad was licking the flavor off his fingers. "We do?"

Kate nodded, making sure that everyone was looking at her. "Tomorrow, no matter what, we are going fishing!"

Everybody laughed and Kate stood there with her hands on her hips. "What?!"

Dad hugged her. "You got it kiddo. We will spend the whole day fishing tomorrow."

They all went to bed, the sounds of monsters spawning and moving around moaning and groaning kept them up for a little bit, but eventually they were able to fall asleep. Morning came and they all woke up, rested and ready for the day.

Dad gave Mom the wool he and Jack had gathered earlier which made her very excited. "Wonderful! I know just how I'll use this!"

"I figured you would, my crafty girl. I'm going to take these two fishing today." Dad kissed her on the cheek and the three of them headed out, leaving Mom to her crafts.

Kate had run off quickly while Jack walked with Dad. "She's sure in a hurry," he said.

Dad nodded and they followed after her. When they got to the pond Kate was wandering around inspecting it. Jack smiled.

"Is something wrong?" Dad asked.

Kate looked up, then shook her head. "No, but it looks like it was fixed so it's not as deep."

Jack raised his hand. "Yep, I did that so no more drowneds would spawn."

Kate rushed over and gave him a hug. "Thanks Jack, tha was so nice!"

Dad looked at Jack with obvious pride and patted him on the shoulder. "Good job son, now let's get our fishing on!" He pulled out his fishing rod and looked at the water, casting in a spot he liked.

"Oh yeah!" Kate shouted and cast her line a bit off from Dad's. Bubbles came and each of them caught something. Dad pulled back and a raw cod flew through the air toward him. Kate pulled back and a pair of leather boots flew out of the water. "What?" she said. "Is this a joke? I don't even get a fish?"

Jack chuckled and Dad handed him the fishing rod for a turn.

"How hard is it to catch a saddle anyway?" Jack asked as they both cast their lines into the water.

Kate watched her bobber intently, not looking away while she answered her brother. "Oh, it's pretty hard. They are really rare. I think it will probably take a super long ti-"

"Got one!" Jack said and he proudly displayed the saddle he had just caught.

Kate looked at him in utter disbelief. "WHAT!?"

Jack gave the fishing rod back to Dad. "I'm just lucky, I guess. Do you want it?"

Kate's face was bright red. "No! I am going to get my own!" She furiously cast her line into the water again.

"Are you sure?" Jack asked, holding out the saddle. "I don't think I'll use it."

Kate turned her nose up to it.

"Just leave her alone Jack, she wants to do it on her own," Dad said.

Jack shrugged. "Well, I'm going to go help Mom then. Fishing is boring."

Dad's mouth dropped open. "Don't you dare say that! I should wash your mouth out with soap!"

"What? It *is* boring!" Jack said.

"You go tell your mother what you said!" Dad pointed towards the house and Jack rolled his eyes and left. When he was gone Dad looked at Kate. "Fishing is NOT boring."

Kate chuckled. "I like it. When there are no drowneds around, it's relaxing."

They continued to fish through the whole day until it was almost nighttime. The sun was low in the sky when Dad and Kate decided it was just about time to quit. They had caught a ton of fish and a few other items, including a set of leather boots for everyone. This time when they pulled back their lines, though, Dad got something unusual. "Hey, I caught a book!"

Chapter 14

Dad looked at the book. It had a thick, fabric cover with ld timey font and a faded picture of an ancient looking astle. It was titled 'World History.'

"Huh," Dad said.

Kate looked at the cover and surprise took over her face. I've never seen anything like that before."

"Let's go show this to Mom. She'll be so happy you kids an read again."

Kate's face fell. "No Dad, please don't! She'll make us ead it all the time and it looks so... boring."

"We don't keep secrets from Mom," he said, and Kate new better than to argue.

When they opened the door of their house, they were hocked at what greeted them.

"Wipe your feet!" Mom yelled as they walked in. Sure enough, at the entrance just outside the door, there was a piece of carpet laid down as a floor mat. They did as she said and went in.

The inside of the house had changed dramatically. During the time Dad and Kate had spent fishing, Mom had extended the house, and using cobblestone, made three individual rooms- one for each kid and one for Mom and Dad. In the area that used to have the beds, there was now a large wooden table with four wooden chairs, one on each side. The dirt floor had been completely dug out and replaced with wood.

"Wow, you've been busy!" Kate said. "How did you make all this?"

Mom beamed at her. "The new walls were easy, but I really wanted some furniture. At first I didn't know what to do, but then Jack," she pointed at Jack who was sitting in one of the new chairs, "showed me that when you place stairs you can turn them whatever way you want. So, I connected stairs to some dirt blocks, upside down, then destroyed the blocks and filled in the gap with wooden slabs to make the table. The chairs are just one block of wooden stairs. Not the most advanced setup, but we needed something so we stop getting crumbs in the beds."

"I knew you'd figure out something amazing honey," Dad said and kissed her on the cheek. "I have something for you." He handed her the book. "Fished it out of the pond today."

Mom just about jumped for joy. "Oh yay! Books! You didn't tell me there were books here, kids. Now you can continue with your lessons!"

"Oh man!" Kate and Jack said at the same time.

"I can't wait to give you homework," Mom said.

"Ugh," Jack and Kate groaned at the same time again.

Dad laughed and sat on one of the new chairs. "Let's take a look at what it says." He opened the book to the first page and began reading.

"Long, long ago, the world was full of many wonderful cities and kingdoms. Monsters were rare and peace was plentiful. The people of the world were able to mine and craft with ease, without worry of what evil lurked around the corner, and many wonderful creations were made.

Fantastic pyramids in the jungles, deserts were places of trade and sport, amazing underwater monuments helped keep the oceans tamed and provided fun places to visit. Mansions throughout the woods offered relaxing places for the people to unwind and enjoy nature. Deep mines and strongholds were built underground to help find the rarest of blocks.

"But then something terrible happened. An explorer found a ruin with a strange broken rectangle made of obsidian. With the help of the greatest miners from all over the world they were able to fix it but could not figure out its purpose. Until late one evening, someone accidentally lit it on fire with flint and steel, and a portal of light opened from its darkness! Out of the portal came strange men, taller than anyone they had ever seen, and made of a mysterious blackness like the dark of night. So dark they seemed to suck the very light from the air."

Everyone sat on the edges of their seat, listening in silent fascination. Apparently Dad paused for too long because Jack said, "What then, Dad? What happened when they came out of the portal?"

Dad continued reading. "Behind them came a powerful witch, a hero, who was hunting the black creatures to send them back where they belonged. Her name was Baba Yaga, and she used her magic to send the strange men made of night, Endermen she called them, back into the portal. Once they had been returned she destroyed the portal, but it was too late, and the world was forever changed.

"Baba Yaga explained that with the opening of the portal, a curse was released onto the world, causing people to turn into zombies, and breaking down the barrier between worlds, allowing Endermen to haunt and attack us. The curse sent out other new monsters into the world to ravage and destroy. She did everything she could to help, but in the end her magic was not strong enough. A terrible beast called the Ender Dragon, a winged creature, dark as the night with wicked purple eyes, escaped through the barrier between worlds and nearly destroyed our lands.

"After many weeks, The Dragon and Baba Yaga faced each other. In a days long, epic battle the likes of which the world had never seen, there emerged no victor. Their power, though opposite, was equal, and both were destroyed.

"The people remained hopeful that with the Ender Dragon gone things could return to normal, but despite Baba Yaga's sacrifice, the curse remains. Monsters continue to plague the lands and our people struggle to rebuild, only able to form tiny villages, poor memories of the great kingdoms of the past.

What will become of the world? Will we ever be free from the curse or will we fall to the darkness? Will another witch ever become powerful enough to save us? Only time will tell."

Dad closed the book and looked at the kids. "Is that the story of Minecraft?"

Kate and Jack looked at each other, then back at Dad and shrugged. "That's the first time I've heard of it," Kate said.

Jack nodded. "Yeah me too. I knew about the dragon, friends from school told me about it. And we've fought Endermen before, they are kinda spooky. But I didn't know any of this stuff."

Kate pulled her legs up and wrapped her arms around them. "It sounds kinda scary. I hope that's just a story and it's not real."

"But if it is real," Jack said, "maybe a witch could help us get back home?"

"That's a good point, Jack." Dad nodded. "Maybe we should try to find one."

"Well I know one thing for sure." Mom looked right at Kate and Jack. "If you can get books from fishing, then that means school is back in session!"

They groaned.

Dad just laughed. "Well I think it's time for bed, tomorrow is a new day with new things to explore."

Kate nodded. "And I'm *finally* going to get my saddle!"

The End!

Thank you for reading our book! We hope you enjoyed reading it as much as we did writing it and that you want to read more!

The idea for The Accidental Minecraft Family came from our own family enjoying playing Minecraft together. How cool would it be if you were actually pulled into the game in real life?! Um, SO COOL!

This book was written by a mom and dad, with tons of help from a daughter who is 10 and a son who is 8. They brainstormed with us, thought of cool ideas, and read the books before they were finished to tell us what parts were good and what jokes were lame. Kids are super smart and creative and have some of the best ideas!

We need your help though! It's a lot of work to write a book, but sometimes the hardest part is finding all the readers. This is where you come in! First of all, tell your friends! You can also help other kids and their parents find our books by leaving a short review. (Make sure to ask your parents first!) It doesn't have to be long, just a few words on why you liked it and pick how many stars you think the book should get (hopefully 5!)

Ours kids get super excited to read every review that comes in, and they even do a little dance. They also would love to hear your favorite parts of the book or if you have anything you would love to see in the next books! So please leave a review, then go read more of our books.

Reading is so cool. You get to sit at home (or in the car or waiting room or wherever you are) and escape to a whole other world without even standing up! Plus, all the scientists say it's good for your brain. And who doesn't want a super-duper smart brain? Read on, friends!

You can get the next book in the series here:

BOOK 3:

Thanks! Hope to see you in the next book!

About the Author(s)

Pixel Ate is actually a team! We're a mom and dad, who live in the Pacific Northwest. We have five kids ages 10 all the way down to 1. We don't like to brag, but we think our kids are the best.

We live on a little bit of land that we're slowly turning into a farm! We like having lots of space outside to run and play and we're excited to fill it with some animals. Yay for goats!

Everyone in our family loves reading- well, the baby loves chewing on books- so we thought, why not write our own stories? It's super fun creating worlds and characters and adventures and even more fun when we know other people are enjoying them. Plus, it's extra special when our kids get to help.

We really did have a cat named Bruce Lee the Scar-Faced Ninja Attack Kitty From Japan (Who Smells Like Poop) who got himself into all kinds of sticky situations, but sadly, he is no longer with us. He truly was a great kitty and he truly did fart a lot. Now we have an equally great kitty named Tater Tot and she is a lot less stinky, but just as loved.

Made in the USA
Coppell, TX
05 November 2020